Life During the Lazarus Age

Other Titles from Space Cowboy Books

Books

Dreaming of Autonomous Vehicles – Jaroslav Olša, Jr.

The Future is Brief – Jean-Paul L. Garnier

Wave IX – Various Authors

The Martians - Emilie Procházková

Mexicans on the Moon – Pedro Iniguez

Another Time: Time Travel Stories 1942–1960 – ed. Jean-Paul L. Garnier

Complete Poems 1965–2020 – Michael Butterworth

Simultaneous Times Vol. 3 – Various Authors

Simultaneous Times Vol. 2.5 – Various Authors

Simultaneous Times Vol. 2 – Various Authors

Simultaneous Times Vol. 1 – Various Authors

Garbage In, Gospel Out – Jean-Paul L. Garnier

Betelgeuse Dimming – Jean-Paul L. Garnier

Future Anthropology – Jean-Paul L. Garnier

Chapbooks

Micropoetry for Microplanets – Brian U. Garrison

Shelf Life – F. J. Bergmann

Mars Maundering – Denise Dumars

The Telepathy Machine – Jean-Paul L. Garnier

Time's Arrow – Jean-Paul L. Garnier

Utopian Problems – Jean-Paul L. Garnier

www.spacecowboybooks.com

Life During the Lazarus Age

Robert Frazier

ISBN 979-8-9896308-7-5

Edited by Jean-Paul L. Garnier
Book design by F. J. Bergmann
Cover image by Bob Eggleton

First Edition | 2025
All Rights Reserved

Space Cowboy Books
61871 29 Palms Hwy.
Joshua Tree, CA 92252
www.spacecowboybooks.com

Contents

IMPRACTICAL MAGIC

WHAT WE KNOW FROM TIME TRAVEL

A Note to Cosmonauts
Addressing Relativistic Concerns

Time will dilate for you
As in the case of Sergei Krivalev
Who zipped around the planet
For 800 days total in ISS orbit
And became a true time-traveler
Leaping two hundredths of a second
Into his personal future
Thus returning a shade younger
Compared to you and everyone

The Veneers of Sleep
At an Excavation of Vietnam

1 The archaeologist

The geology of his sweat lacquered skin
is a uniform marbling of ochre and more ochre,
the dirt so impregnating the cells' thin
walls that he can't wash it away at all
in the plant-iron kettle of tepid water
he heats by his computerized lean-to at dusk.
Perhaps the golden soil enters the blood and bone,
the finest yellow of remembered tiger hairs,
rain forest plumage, fruit husks,
that even the sluicing won't settle down.
This is how the craving for the truth grows,
one as powerful as his brother's for Space,
as adrenalin fires in his veins like lava flows
aglow on a nearby mist-shrouded cone.
Perhaps this is what torches the ganglia
and begins a slow excavation of his obsession.

2 *The pit*

Carrying dirt bags, loaves of dripping bread,
the scientist humps his way up ladder poles
made stable with fraying lengths of cable.
He sloughs them off to his helpers at the top
as if the bags were sins for confession,
acknowledged and then ignored.
This man's natural bronze is leached
pale by constant puckering from the sluice slop.
He turns, gazing back into the hole, the checkerboard
of uneven village foundations and temple rubble,
and realizes this was his last load of the day.
The air in the jungle has a musty smell,
the scent of a foul gas that bubbles
up from the bowels of the continent.
At the rim, where workers are still visible,
the sky hangs pink, the thinnest wash of blood.
Deep down, at the lowest levels, bodies empurple,
become dark smudges beneath a grim veneer.
He peers at their sweaty backs winking
in the sinking late afternoon sun
like the gleam of pyrite in a fool's eye.

3 *His home*

Back at the lean-to, he boils his bath
and a pot for the strong drink
which uplifts his blood from simple rust.
He wipes his hands on the brown of his khakis
and his face on a blown-out bag he once used
as a filter mask against the merciless dust.
From his pocket he removes a slim pink slip,
a read-out from the Cao Dai government
for a six-month extension of his project.
He adds it to a cigar box filled with checks
and other bits, worn letters from his family.
He watches a strip of black plastic
skitter by like a low-flying bat.
He lays out across his cot
his hat and clean clothes for a trip
down into the busy plaza.
He is careful, patient, and without thought.

4 *The Plaza of Myths*

Other scientists, miners of the past
talk excitedly of a helicopter found,
of excavation fatalities, of pilots who soar
through the Central Highlands to bring fresh
supplies and tools from provincial capitals.
The archaeologist strolls like a tourist
drinking in conversation as bright as
novae, as a wizard's elixir, as visions
of lost and indecipherable cultures.
There's a crowd around a veteran,
a man who discovered a full battle site,
yet he talks as if the mass grave is between
his eyes — the man's voice is haunted.
His teeth are filled with grains of gold
flashing like constellations to the south,
and within gleams some mystical pattern
of warrior's dreams, of souls bought and sold.
So the archaeologist, like some dumb tourist
lost in the droning voice, the golden mouth,
feels like he's flying on reconnaissance.
And it seems like he's been riding out
on the sound of gunfire in his brain.

5 A nightly ritual

All of a sudden he misses his family;
it's an acid that boils up in his throat.
He leaves the Plaza of Myths, climbs the hill
up to the trails leading to his sleep site.
Even through the fog-misted sky above,
he feels the needles of actinic starlight,
hears the air compressors and sluice pumps.
Opening the door flap, he gropes in the dark,
finds a glow stick and the letters from home.
He unfolds them slowly, flattens their creases
as if he were stroking long silken hair,
reads aloud about his brother at Luna Base 9,
a sister lost in a shuttle crash,
and his mother back in Quang Tri, in despair.
Whether it's death-talk that has dried up his glands
or the rust and gold running through his head,
he won't shed a single tear, just steps outside
and stares straight into the darkness overhead
to where the alternate light, the light of past years,
flees to the fringes of heaven.
And when his eyes can take no more strain
he crawls at last to his hard bed.

6 Envoi

It seems like he's been gliding
above his body where it sleeps,
and it seems like he's flying high,
skirting his blood-stained dreams.

Robert Frazier

Here Is What Is Lost to Me

The sensory taste of honey.
The buoyancy of the sea.
I traded my beating heart
For a faintly murmuring pump
And a pink hemoglobin goo.
I reduced my familial ties
To links to dated holovids,
Or rare offworld meet-ups
With elderly descendants.
I gave up on immediacy.
But the things truly lost,
Now that I am anchored
By planetary gravity once more,
Are the reasons for these forfeits.
The wonder of alien lives.
The great nothingness out there.
The ache for becoming just more.
The words for simple truths.

Maintenance Subroutine: Sanity

His skull smoldered with white heat
radiant signatures of the galactic arm
as he floated in the sensory chamber

    her voice a filament of hope
    insinuated along old frequencies
    first imprinted by her touch

his phantom heart throbbed
like a limb lost but not lost
within his tech-scarred chest

    her voice moved through the chaos
    through his veins of artificial blood
    as calming as a narcotic

his memory raveled in flower symmetries
images of her face became exotic tastes
taste buds held extinct languages

    her voice no longer spoke
    it matched the rhythm in his spine
    the synaptic flares of his thoughts

his self relaxed back into the matrices
the piloting routines and controls
as the lightship held to course

The Phantom Navigator in Stasis

I dreamt last cycle of Mandalay station
Made of inky fins & blinking ports
A packet rife with babble

The hydrogen haloes of the Crab Nebula
Spun into a swirling axle of creation
About Mandalay's image in my vidscreen

Remote docking went without incident
But my sub exited into a still node
No greeters no status boards no lifeforms

The emptiness spoke with silence
Just a cavity of need and I awoke
Frozen in a gravity-less trance

This note is the black box recovery
Of what I saw of what I thought I saw
Of none of that and how it matters

Schwarzschild Never Predicted This

Orbiting your black nothingness
Beyond the triple grav radius
Of your lightless influence,
My chest balls with lightning.
Blood sluices boldly
As my arteries tsunami.

A magnet never requires iron.
And lips don't need other lips.
Yet I yearn for the full
Of your consumptive pull.

I was born with your hole,
Supermassive and remote,
Ghosted and once lost within
My many-chambered heart.

Robert Frazier

When I Heard the Learn'd Astrophysicist

after Walt Whitman

Her NASA socks ripped at one toe,
Just to the edge of Saturn.
Her coelacanth tee bore a hole.
I think you spot the pattern.
She wore science on her sleeve,
That forever threatened to tatter,
And hoped before she takes her leave
To suss the "damn truth" on dark matter.

The Lovesong of **A. *afarensis* Lucy**

after T. S. Eliot

There you go then
With your skeleton
Spread out and numbered,
Just a hominid tumbled upon a table.
Your life now just smoke that slides
Across decades of discoveries.

While in the museum at Addis Ababa
Paleoanthropologists come and go on
Talking of the Leakeys.

Indeed they'll make the time
To mold your model, mimic your face.
There will be days of handiwork long long
After your 3-million-years-ago time.
Hasn't it been worthwhile to wait
So long in that dry stony gully.

Paleoanthropologists come and go,
Yet you remain in bones.
A mother to everyone.

Life On the Low Road

Beneath the behemoth skyscrapers
We survive in deep shadow

For those of us in rebellious clans
A soft target anxiety permeates

Polscans pass like ball lighting
Hovering low and soundless

Hunting any free thinkers along
With eye-in-the-sky hover cams

While underground cartels trade ideas
While progressives hide among the tombs

And while one water vendor stands proud
Chants in the square facing upwards

Begging for a beam of pure sunlight
To fall between the towers

Or calling for a salvation of weather
To flood his hidden catch basins

His daughter beckons to buyers
With psychotropic holograms

She snaps her gloved fingers
And sparks morph to rain drops

Memories based on simpler freer times
Seem to coalesce in the air as well

Then wink out like the stars
Now long dead to our viewing

Life During the Lazarus Age

The invasion starts with taxa known to reappear.
The lobe-finned coelacanth considered extinct
Since the Cretaceous then rediscovered in 1938
Is caught in droves along the Jersey shore.
Lord Howe Island stick bugs down to a dozen left
Now in swarms vex Kew Gardens tourists.
Then extinct total newcomers flood back in.
Dodos colonize Maui and Oahu pineapple groves.
Ankylosaurus routs the 'cocaine hippos' from Colombia.
Two passenger pigeons stow away on a moon mission.
And a *Gigantopithecus* climbs the Empire State tower
At dawn and bellows a warning to generations soon
To be overrun by the 99.9% of all species that ever lived.

Our Quantum Detective Works Her Board

Aware of her own ambiguities
As a cloned operative undercover,
Our DCI voices a quip while sussing out
Theories upon her virtual white board:
"You can't be in two places at once."
Yet she scrawls in luminous marker:
By quantum information theory the state
Of a particle can be replicated at
A distance from its relative location.
Then red highlights: *relative.*
So she challenges the incident room.
"If we can isolate every particle
Of our bodies then replicate elsewhere,
Can our suspect be temporally dual?"
Her lead DI: "You mean teleportation.
That's just no good of course
Without a plan on the other end
To put Humpty together again."
Another DI: "And after could you/they
Truly be the exact same person."
Our DCI writes out, *Can we prosecute a copy?*
Which of them would be the guilty party?
But what she's really thinking is
—I'm leading a dual life here on duty.—
Like the two-state qubit with a value
Of one or zero depending on the spin,
What outcome will she end up in?
Accepted or rejected.

What We Know Now from Time Travel

Time heals no wounds
But makes an effective bandage

It's easy to find heartbreak
In truly long distance relationships
No killing father no marrying mother

You can't be a self-made man
Wait a day for tomorrow is the limit
That you can travel into the future
Living in the present is relative
So is living in the far distant past

I'm somewhere you're somewhere
We both hold to no fixed line

Time beats on a madman's drum
Plays our souls in crosstime measures

Stake Out

The light-pierced curvature of dusk lifts its skirt
birds are spinning on the latticework
of wired antennae
and a ribbon of dried utterance
flaps decorously from each
a blindness that says I told you so
yes, I know … all the chances ever missed

And across surrounding docking bays
hard yet smooth as flesh
a mercurial rain pools into flowing mirrors
the buildings fracture and reform
like the memory of
some embrace

Oh I see her now defying gravity
my unknowing Martian love
her hair tilted into the matter stream
waiting for the last souls to depart
so that she may depart
vertical to Antares yet never further
than what she must call home

Why have I traveled this far
to feed on my own reflection
to sit in the iron vessel of myself
and dream possibility
I will forget everything
nothing

My Yesterdays Haven't All Happened Yet

I've survived
Dozens of birthdays.
Died so so many times
That I can't remember.
And who would want to.
Once came out *Homo habilis*.
Shattered all my femurs thrice.
Had my heart broken far more.
Yeah it's a bright size life alright,
Yet … all this I never cease to outlive.

A Caution: On Being One of the Invisibles

Sure, the Future City looks less crowded.
Invisibility has its downsides though.
Naked, unadorned, you can't see your feet
While hologram ads dance around you.
You must careen into the tube rails
Where riders notice boxes and barstools
That move on their own but shrug these
Off as just another aerosol drug mirage.
Oh and the winters trapped in clothing,
Mummy-wrapped like a burn victim,
When you actually have to pay for things.
Yet if the cloaking effect wavers for a bit,
When you're happy to be seen again,
Dolled up to cruise the street raves,
Well then no one notices you anyways
With their billion eyes averted, resigned
Within their own prisons of anonymity.

Erasure

We first took notice when we noticed less:
they stayed in the peeling antebellum manse,
attending no town meetings, or cotillions.
The three misanthropic brothers worked only
as wizards of hack, plucking their histories
from Georgia's data banks, the FBI, IRS,
catalog mailing lists as far off as Indonesia.
Slowly, the old bamboo patch walled them.
Mail trickled to nothing, like a desert wadi.
Eventually, telephone lines they used were dismantled.
On the night they vanished, the auroras danced
in veils of vermillion, sent streamers down like
fishing jigs to touch the dew-dropped magnolias.
In the morning we found the grounds seamless
and so green where once the foundation stood.

Now That I Have Found You

Before I knew where I was
I was already lost to it.
We had jumped in so close.
I turned back to the vid screen.
There it/she was in immense reveal.
So familiar an exoplanet yes so alive.
Landforms like Earth but not Earth.
And those ocean hues of blues.
We had jumped to a sure match.
I felt the rush of a heart swell,
Like when a brutal wormhole
Tugs you through to the impossible.
Like when love slays you dumb.
So familiar yes yet how could
Something this immensely right
Ever be just a match to the past.
Ever be considered ordinary.
I was already lost.

Adagio for the Lost Mutant Rain Forest

Deep within the least-known Amazon,
By the Rio dos Mutantes headwaters,
Tall thickets of buttressed *Ceiba pentandras*
Have stood a millennia of summers as
Survivors in a dwindling patch of rain forest.
Just one of their sweeping canopies
Constitutes an entire ecosystem.
The luminous decay of a mycelial network lights
The underbellies of their elephant ear bromeliads.
MechBee escapees from the cities harvest
The psychotropic saps of the Pavonine flower.
Barb-tailed sloths articulate staccato calls.
And cloudbursts rattling their topmost layers
Release those sweet floral fragrances that
Compel every creature to colonize their grove.
A single traveler entrapped by this siren snare
Now lives along a garretted catwalk which
Circumferences a giant among these giants,
And she adds her fluting throat songs
To the seductive green voice of the trees.

Syllabus for the Modern Dryad

While the climate degrades more humans
Than ever transfigure to tree nymphs

You can tell a triplet or quintuplet tree
By the burl-like cluster of nymph nodes

An orphaned nymph suffers bitter exile
From the forest to the open glens

A nihilist hamadryad inhabits
A curiously unidentifiable arboreal species

The Llorona dryad creaks limbs
Rattles a brittle chain of leaflets

And dryads of the burning Amazon jungle
Conjure a wind of deep melancholia

YOUR CLONE

Your Clone Authors a Sticky Note

If a clone is cloned again
and then again for generations
does the heart weaken the soul bleach
like a color print that fades a bit
each morning in the sunlight

Your Clone Finds Her Stray

She searches where you didn't
through the sluiceways of the Belt
to a back station of ore jockeys

and down in the pitted warrens
where water condensers grind
and air tastes dull with waste gases

your clone susses out her lost sister
using your morphology as a code
a shared face as a tracking device

when they meet their embrace runs
gravity tight and teary-eyed
oh what bones must this one bury

how did this forgotten girl sleep
so far off grid so far from her family
and your clone wonders most

who last whispered her real name

Your Clone Speaks with the Ancients

There is little in her voicing
That hints at a tragedy
Or at instability in her hippocampi
Your clone babbles out coherence
From her place beside your others
And if you can parse
The sibilance and the cadence
There's a still point to explore there
A calm to occupy beside her
As she sways inside the Call
So linger and take the same risk
You can almost discern a response
Some past lifelines of you
Whistling back
From that big sky country

Robert Frazier

Your Clone Hones Telepathy

When you all gather for your luncheon
In the garden cackling like crows
Your newest clone seems conspicuous
Despite the obvious similarities

Her silence betrays her efforts
Face so flushed and immobile
Then you feel her word shapes
That tickling in your thought stream

This time it sharpens and grows
Together you sense a breakthrough
A hint of the time when the only sound
Will be the conference call of real birds

Your Clone Aims to Disremember

If only I could relive redo
The moment I ripped our photograph
Wrenched out of that mental state
That joined us since emergent birth
Now nothing is simple like before
Lost to a war of head and heart
What use is the individual
My savior my destroyer
My world my bond gone
I act and react and act again
Gravity holds me to ground
But the voices of my clone sisters
That were all my own voice
That always rang true
Remain silenced

Your Clone Can Always Look Herselves Up

Like hoarding a jacket of a lost child
And breathing in the odor the absence
This is how a holomemory ensnares
The hungering mind with dimension
With their spirit and their familiar form
How can she tire of this sensation
And with a menagerie at her recall
Past generations might fuse and unify
With just the risk of her total immersion
How difficult to press delete all

Impractical Magic

William Carlos Williams Variation #2

We have cloned
the child
that slept in
your cryobox

in which mankind's
survival hopes
were no doubt
resting

forgive us
improving our odds
seemed too delicious
to pass up

Primer to Impractical Magic

Love Mojo Gone Wrong

It's an easy mojo to tag upon your man
(albeit in a red flannel bag in your boot)

write his name nine times in blood ink and
twine with his hair about a John the Conqueror root

sprinkle on pure Come to Me Stay With Me Oil
you might add a Queen Elizabeth root to be sure

but if there's a shift in spelling a vowel unsteady
or your handwriting drifts or gets rough

you might have two besotted Smiths at the ready
worse … an entire male generation in the buff

counter mojo: use Chase Away Oil erase names

Love Potion Number 9.5

Besides dosing with both eyes of newt
and a big pinch of Ma's Organic Loveroot

the dead-giveaway clue that you've wibbletated
the brew in the alchemist's laundry room

is how anything it even lightly touches
discolors like a lovebite from a vacuum

and you're left stalking cute cops cute perps
or their no-so-cute vics inside the chalk lines

you're just outright kissing frogs or
dog-licking moms on 34th & Vine

full remedy: take two regretamine

Love Wish Voodoo Marks

With a doll—there's a cross of swamp oak inside
and the tear-soaked stuffing of Spanish moss

the pins only affix and direct the slow hex
like the Xs on the tomb of Marie Laveau

with her mausoleum —you place a pattern
you can't just deface it any which way

three red marks in St. Louis Cemetery
then she grants a love wish a bit of fun

but should you pin or X a forbidden spot
you might reverse the structure of your plot

the re-reversal: a kiss on Bayou Loup-garou

Within You and Without You

We are born with 270 individual bones
We die with 60 less
This is not a human quandary

45 thousand millennia of development
From fish to forensic reconstructions
Your skeleton is just hard hard tissue
Able to be stripped down and
Reabsorbed by osteoclasts

Yet able to rebuild from harsh damage
This too lacks mystery

But bone marrow forms red blood
To truck oxygen along
The 9 zillion freeways of the flesh
So why do we worship the heart muscle
Why do we romanticize it
It only pumps platelets and cells
And when love breaks the heart
There is no power to heal the damage
Only a gloomy jukebox lament
Plus the salve of time

Robert Frazier

Amor Machina

We circled each other
like koi swimming
through the heavens
her neoprene smile
radiated solar wind
from a trillion polymers
the dialects of her
insinuation grew
until it was language
murmurations punctuating
my anxious night visions
while the press of her lips
left coded messages
of bold-faced lies
and I believed every one
for her artifice
was bliss

Your Dark Angel

Your dark angel swims in blue lightning
Through the ice fields of your dream

She kisses heat waves into your slack lips
And brings sight to your blind core

She whispers sin from every speaker
A suggestion you can almost hear

She speaks jihad from the wasteland
Of numberless television news clips

She screams fire from the air raid sirens
In a whitewash of static hiss

She watches you from the sky drones
Maps your course through the day

She peeks at you through all lenses
Mimics your moves like a shadow

She blinks from the LED screens
With undecipherable error messages

She paints hidden directives
On the periphery of your vision

Your dark angel divines your probables
Unravels massive streams of binary

Your dark angel parses your red truths
Unravels the never-has-been

Your dark angel knows you
Like no other will ever ever know you

Red Truths

Speaking strictly for me
In that storm during Martian summer
On the flanks of Olympus Mons
I felt a definite sea change
Now I'm caught in your undertow

Dark dust battered our faceplates
While the syrups of our imperiled souls
Co-mingled so sweetly that day
Our voices statically whispering the verity
Of our circumstance in our heads

Now you're lost in the North Polar Basin
Out of radio contact
I leave the lights in the air locks
Permanently on full burn
And await your return

Oh, My Inamorata/Inamorato

They who cages your heart in wires of black ice
They who tases you with a crackling fire of need
They who forwards your despair to the hotline of oblivion
Who texts prayers that ratchet through your fevers
Who scans your cerebellum with fluoroscopic sight
Whose larynx keens a blizzard of siren vowels
Whose graphene hips cast typhoons with a thrust
Whose touch stains you with addictive alkaloid inks
They who asks no fealty
They who you must obey

Aftereffect

If teleportation were an ecstasy,
the fortunately gifted would
zip zip zip from present to present.

Thus time travel sans a future to reach…
and where the baggages of their pasts
wash clean with each jaunt,
leaving a purity of the now.

A breathless moment on the red plains of Mars.
A freefall from the frigid heights of the ionosphere.
A nanosecond of absolute heat at the Sun's core.

Teleporters might share these pleasures
if they could only escape the thought
that with every cleansing leap
they must await the *tabula rasa*
of inevitable uncreation,
of identity without context.

Here Is What You Must Do

First study weather study the outworld races
win the anthropology chair but refuse

ship out to the snow planet of Altair 4
when the expedition drives north you go

when the storm wall looms you dig not run
after you claw your way to the surface

the winds still howl the snows blow you wait
she will pass then return with a covered sled

she will tend you in her igloo with thick stews
when you emerge from the heat of delirium

you will find you did not study her dialect
and she cannot fathom a syllable of yours

yet the next word she utters you must learn
and cherish as her name until the end of days

Dragons Discover Fire

Out of pyrocumulus clouds
Caught in great storm whirl
The flight of dragons settles
In a forest scorched barren
When a fire tornado
Lashes about them
Panting with difficulty
They inhale raw flame
Breathe out raw flame
Inhale more exhale more
And a legend is born
Passed down generations
As the young learn to store
Solids gases and plasma
Learn the ignition points
To their incandescent lives

The Temple Necromanteion

after the oil painting "Isle of the Dead"
by Arnold Böcklin (1827–1901)

Ferried before these ruined walls,
the mourner bound in white linen
bids her boatman to raise his oar.

They transport the body of Charon,
a frequent visitor though he never set
a boot on these granite steps.

She chants in tongues of necromancy.
A stiff breeze offers reply as it threads
through black spears of cypress.

She launches his sarcophagus adrift
to surf into shallows and land high
on a shore of bleached bones.

From steep cliffs glazed with rain,
cries of harpies and hellhounds
sweep away to the world above.

It's Always All About the Weather
in Greenfield, Iowa

If I were the calm before the storm
My brain pan would crackle
With lightning strikes of recall
My worries form a distant thunder
My soul in a plains twister rotation
Would tear the door hinges off
Museums of my precognition
I would be the canary in the mine
A forecaster of future weathers
If I were the calm before the storm

Salinity

Sweating in the full glare of August,
my father taught me a bittersweet truth
on a beach day, when he was restless
to be holding something
other than me—
a surf casting rod perhaps,
or the glow of health that eluded him and
corroded year by year like his station wagon
from halite poured on New England's icy roads.
He taught me that we preserved our heritage,
our only heritage really,
in the saltiness of our blood.
A striped bass can't live out of the sea,
he said, or in fresh water either.
Yet we carry our oceans with us from birth to beyond.
And as he cut short this speech,
fully knowing what carcinomas ate at him,
he let tears drop into the sea spraying on me.
Unmindful, I sucked the salt from my wrist.
Now they haunt my veins
those molecules of his within me,
that ocean within the head of a pin.
There whole ecologies of salinity,
of the evolution of things
once left unsaid,
await evaporation and condensation
and distillation.
Worlds reduced within worlds.
Lives within lives.
Yesterdays.

The Void Where Our Hearts Used To Be

I've seen the best Void Runners of my generation
scarred, vectorless, tired of the emptiness
yet always craving the vastness

who were scrapped like fried jump-drive parts
who are still hooked on those stormy dynamos
those machineries of flight

who bay at the moons the suns the obscuring dust
waiting waiting to be transfixed and spread far
like passengers cryosealed upon a table

and when the change comes
the true weight of the multitude of lives
we have lived and burned will balance to zero

when the change comes
our Klein bottle souls will reinvert
make revisions to the vain yearnings we contain

and, yes, when the change truly comes
the oxygenating machines in our chests
will shiver in blue-shifted beats

charting us back from all the far neutopias
bridging the void the deserted streets
where our torn-out hearts used to be

Final Dispatch

Out where the stars thrum in shortwave
Who'll find this lightship set adrift
Sweep the cosmic dust from my grave
Hoist out my black box treasure trove
Restore the burnt core of my love

No more code to thread and rethread
No new ideas to drive through my head
So discharge my soul in section eight
Convert me to transcendental matter
Lord let me die in an ionized state

Epicenter

A faint rumble, the desk shakes, an echo.
Adrenalized, my hands falter above the notebook
keyboard and begin to enter a new line:
"A faint rumble, the desk shakes …"
It's as if earthquakes follow the physics
In a bubble chamber, where atoms are altered
or decayed. I collapsed from balancing
my checkbook into this poem, this echo.

Acknowledgements

Works first appeared in:

Altered Reality, Alternate Lives, Amazing Stories, Analog Science Fiction & Fact, Asimov's Science Fiction, Dreams and Nightmares, Eye to the Telescope, The Magazine of Fantasy and Science Fiction, Midwest Futures (Middle West Press), *SFPA Valentines Day Page, Speculative Poetry Review, Silver Blade, Star*Line, Strange Horizons, The Heartbeat of the Universe* (Interstellar Flight Press), *The Rhysling Anthology*

Original to this collection:

"Schwarzschild Never Predicted This"

"Your Clone Speaks With the Ancients"

Also by Robert Frazier

Speculative Poetry Anthology, editor

Burning With a Vision, Owlswick Press, 1984

Poetry Collections

Perception Barriers, Berkeley Poets Workshop & Press, 1987

Co-Orbital Moons, Ocean View Books, 1987

Chronicles of the Mutant Rain Forest, with Bruce Boston, Horror's Head Press, 1992

Invisible Machines, Jazz Police Books, with Andrew Joron, 1993

The Daily Chernobyl and Other Poems, Anamnesis Press, 2000

Phantom Navigation, Dark Regions Press, 2012

Visions of the Mutant Rain Forest, with Bruce Boston, Crystal Lake Publishing, 2017

Chapbooks

Peregrine, Salt-Works Press, 1978

A Measure of Calm, with Andrew Joron, The Ocean View Press, 1985

Family Secrets, Eel Grass Press, 1993

ABOUT THE AUTHOR

ROBERT FRAZIER is a founding member of the Science Fiction & Fantasy Poetry Association. He acted as editor/associate editor for the SFPA *Star*Line* journal from issue 4/1 through issue 14/1, plus the earliest *Rhysling Anthologies*. He has been honored with three Rhysling Awards for both long and short poems, and was designated an SFPA Grandmaster in 2005. He also was the 2013 SFPA Poetry Contest winner. He treasures 2 *Asimov's* Readers Poll Awards for poetry.

Nominations include Nebula Awards (for fiction), *Locus* Awards, *Analog* Readers Poll, Balrog Awards, Bram Stoker Awards, Dwarf Stars Awards, *Asimov's* Readers Poll, Rhysling Awards, Anamnesis Press book contest (won in 2000). Poems reprinted in the Nebula Awards Anthology, *Year's Best Science Fiction Annual*, and *Year's Best Fantasy and Horror Annual*.

Bob edited the speculative poetry anthology *Burning With a Vision*, 1984; and also edited the 1970s speculative poetry magazine *Speculative Poetry Review/T.A.S.P.* His ten poetry collections include *Perception Barriers, Phantom Navigation, The Daily Chernobyl, Invisible Machines* (in collaboration with Andrew Joron) and *Visions of the Mutant Rain Forest* (in collaboration with Bruce Boston).

Bob lives on Nantucket Island, working as Artistic Director for Artists Association of Nantucket, with a 50-year career as an oil painter.

About the Artist

BOB EGGLETON has won 9 Hugo Awards, and various other important awards for his art over the last 30 years of his career. He has designed concepts for *Star Trek, Jimmy Neutron Boy Genius* (2001) and *The Ant Bully* (2006) as well as created art for various publishers, magazines, book covers and media projects. His passion is with classic masters of art such as JMW Turner, John Martin, and the Romantic movement. Bob has always been fascinated with 'scale' as a philosophy in the painted image, whether it be the vastness of outer space, or the size of a kaiju, an H. P. Lovecraft denizen, or a dragon viewed from a human perspective. *Spacewatch* named Asteroid 13562 Bobeggleton in his honor. He won the 2015 Rondo Award for Best Artist in Classic Horror.

SPACE
COWBOY